A First-Start® Easy Reader

This easy reader contains only 51 different words,
repeated often to help the young reader develop
word recognition and interest in reading.

Basic word list for *Dinosaur in Trouble*

are	once	Dinny
a	was	dinosaur
his	town	Chief
the	day	name
in	night	lived
and	who	every
but	went	snored
so	that	snoring
he	work	animals
up	worked	people
one	played	until
I	long	cannot
is	loud	blankets
it	woke	pillows
on	sleep	water
did	said	there
not	now	awake

Dinosaur in Trouble

Written by Sharon Gordon

Illustrated by Paul Harvey

Troll Associates

ISBN 0-89375-274-6

10   9   8   7

Once there was a dinosaur.

Dinny was his name.

Dinny the dinosaur lived in town.

Dinny worked in town.

Dinny played in town.

Every day, _____

Dinny worked and played.

But every night,

Dinny snored and snored!

Dinny snored long.

Dinny snored loud.

Dinny snored so long and so loud,

he woke up the town!

He woke up the animals.

He woke up the people.

Until one night,

Dinny woke up the Chief.

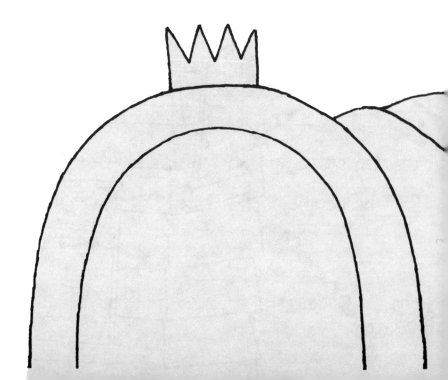

"I cannot sleep," said the Chief.

"Who is snoring so loud?"

"It is Dinny," said the people.

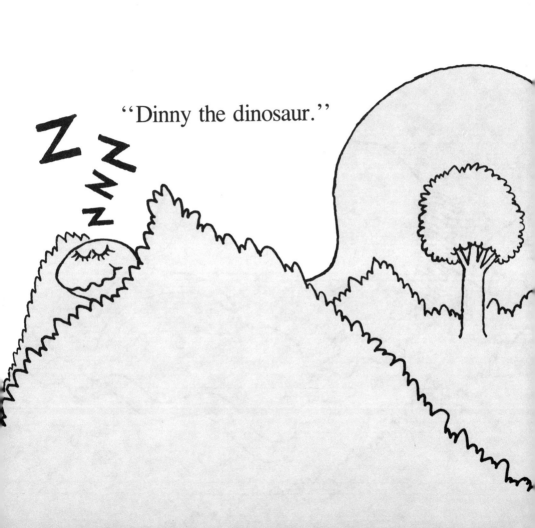

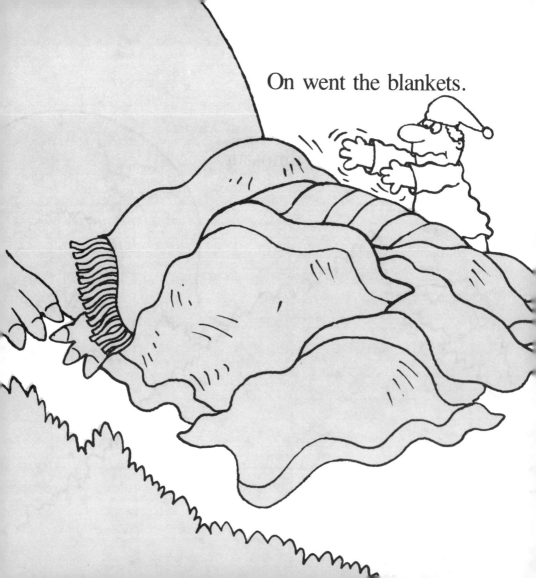

On went the blankets.

That did not work.

On went the pillows.

That did not work.

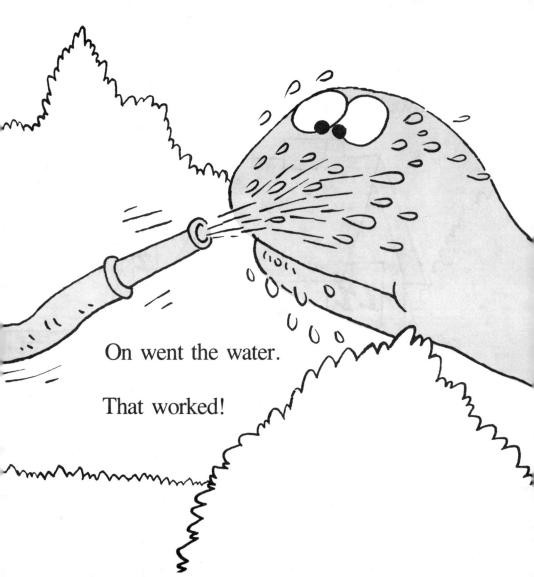

On went the water.

That worked!

Now the people are snoring.

And Dinny is awake!